D0477444

About this book

Many children have difficulty puzzling out letters because they are abstract symbols. Letterland's worldwide success is all about its enduring characters who give these symbols life and stop them from being abstract. In this book we meet Zig Zag Zebra. Her story is carefully designed to emphasise the sounds that the letter 'Z' makes in words. This definitive, original story book is an instant collector's classic, making learning fun for a new generation of readers.

A TEMPLAR BOOK

This edition published in the UK in 2008 by Templar Publishing
an imprint of The Templar Company plc,
The Granary, North Street, Dorking, Surrey, RH4 1DN, UK
www.templarco.co.uk

First published by Thomas Nelson & Sons Ltd, 1993
Devised and produced by The Templar Company plc

1 3 5 7 9 8 6 4 2

ISBN 978-1-84011-787-5

Printed in China

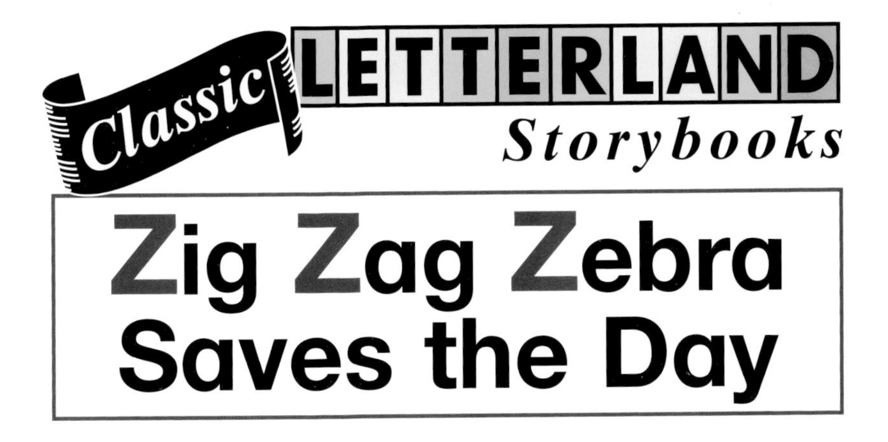

Written by Stephanie Laslett

Illustrated by
Jane Launchbury

templar publishing

Max was sitting on the Letterland School wall, watching the school clock.
"Six minutes to the start of school," he said to himself.

Suddenly a voice yelled "Yoo, hoo!" It was the Yo-Yo Man. He had a bright yellow yo-yo whizzing up and down on a string from his finger.

"I am practising," he explained. "I want to beat the Letterland record for the longest ever go with a yo-yo."

MAX
LETTERL
SCHOO

"I would like everyone to come and watch," said the Yo-Yo Man. "But I haven't time to invite them all."

"Maxine and I will be happy to help," said Max. "We will fix everything."

At that moment Maxine was in the school bell tower. Today it was her turn to ring the bell. Max hoped she was ready because the big hand of the clock was nearly on the 12.

MAX

Maxine *was* ready. All the children loved taking turns to ring the school bell at the start and end of each school day.

Maxine held the rope in both hands. When the clock showed exactly nine o'clock she pulled hard.

"Ding, dong." She pulled again.
"Ding, dong."
"One more pull," she said to herself, but this time the bell made a quite different sound.
"Ding, clang!" it went.

Everyone rushed to the bell tower to see what was wrong.
"Look!" cried Maxine, pointing to the bell. There was a large crack running down one side.

"The bell is broken. It will have to be fixed," she said.

"That will be extremely expensive," said Max. "We must think of a way to raise money to buy a new one."

He thought about how Maxine had pulled on the rope. Down and up it went. It reminded him of something. Something on a string going down and up.

"Of course!" Max cried. "It's the Yo-Yo Man!" He explained all about the yo-yo challenge. "If everyone in Letterland pays him some money for each hour he keeps yo-yoing, we may raise enough to buy a new school bell." Everyone thought that was an excellent idea.

Over the next few days Max and Maxine were extremely busy. They sent out sixty invitations. Maxine drew a lovely poster in wax crayons and fixed it to the school gate. Max put out sixty chairs in the school hall. Soon everything was ready.

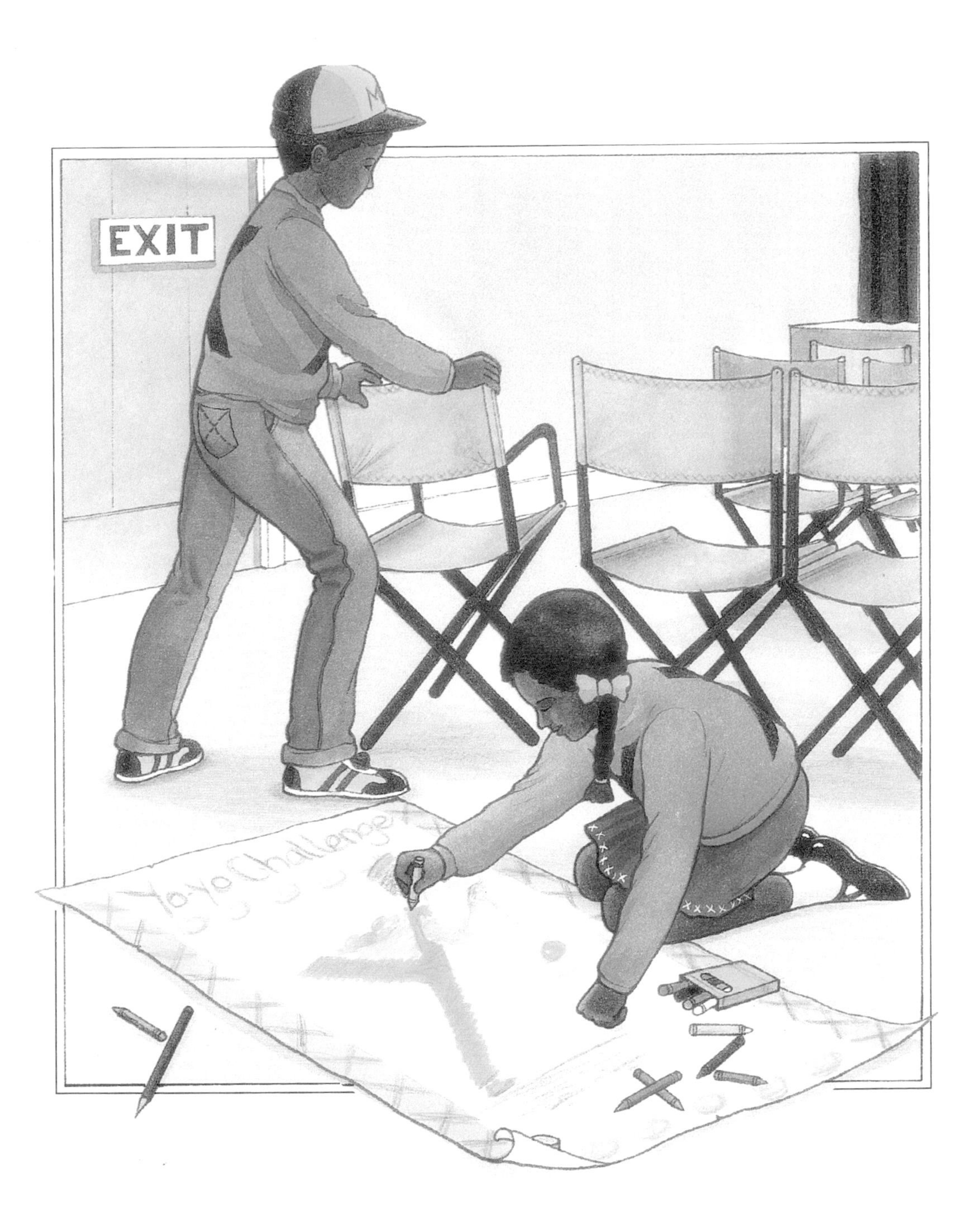
EXIT
Yo-yo Challenge

On the day of the Yo-Yo challenge everyone was very excited. As people arrived, Maxine wrote their names in her exercise book. She wrote down the amount of money they promised to pay if the Yo-Yo Man beat the yo-yo record.

There were so many people that Max had to find extra chairs. At 12 o'clock he gave the countdown.

"The Yo-Yo Man has to keep going for six hours," he cried. "Six, five, four, three, two, one. Go, yo-yo, go!"

The Yo-Yo Man was off. His yo-yo whizzed up and down so fast that it was just a yellow blur. For the first hour he did well, but by one o'clock he was slowing down.

"How can we help him keep going?" everyone wondered.

Max and Maxine fed him with chocolate kisses from a silver box. "Yummy," said the Yo-Yo Man and that kept him going until two o'clock. Jumping Jim gave a jelly juggling display. That helped until three o'clock but then the Yo-Yo Man started to feel dizzy.

CHOCOLATE KISSES

Fireman Fred turned a fan on to cool him down. That worked until four o'clock. But when Fred turned the fan on harder to cool him more, its wind nearly tangled his yo-yo string.

"Sstop, sstop!" hissed Sammy Snake. "I will sing to him instead."

That helped until five o'clock but then the Yo-Yo Man started to look sleepy.

"Look out!" cried Lamp Lady Lucy. "You're singing a lullaby. The Yo-Yo Man is yawning!"

Everyone did what they could to keep him awake, but by sixteen minutes to six they had run out of ideas. The only one who hadn't helped yet was Zig Zag Zebra. She was too shy.

"You could save the day, Zig Zag," said Maxine. "Just tell him your favourite jokes. He can't laugh and yawn at the same time."

"But I'm so shy," whispered Zig Zag. "Can I hide behind the curtains while I tell them?" So Zig Zag hid behind the stage curtains and began to tell her jokes.

MAX

"What's black and white and red all over?" she began.
Everyone was puzzled.
Nobody knew the answer.
"A blushing penguin!" said Zig Zag Zebra. They all laughed and laughed and the Yo-Yo Man laughed loudest of all.

"What goes 'Now you see me, now you don't?'" asked Zig Zag. They all tried hard to think of the answer but she had to tell them.
"A snowman on a zebra crossing!"

Zig Zag went on.
"What's black and white and goes round and round?" Nobody knew.
"A panda in a revolving door!" said Zig Zag.

The Yo-Yo Man roared with laughter. His yo-yo speeded up and was going faster than ever. "Yippee!" he yelled. "It's six o'clock!" Loud cheers filled the air as he broke the record. Now there would be enough money to buy a new school bell.

"But who was the mystery joke teller?" asked the Yo-Yo Man. "Who really saved the day?"

Suddenly Zig Zag Zebra didn't feel shy any more. She came out from behind the curtain and happily took a bow, even though it made her feel black and white – and red – all over!

THE END